Secret Insurrection

Stories from a Novel of a Future Time

Stephani Maari Booker

Athena Persephoni Publications

2018

Second Printing: 2018

This booklet contains fiction that has been previously published, as noted at the end of each story.

ISBN-print: 978-1-7335170-1-0

Athena Persephoni Publications
Minneapolis, MN 55411

www.mnartists.org/smbooker

Contents

Secret Insurrection:
An End and a Beginning

"Lydia! Lydia! Girl, where are you?" Lydia Ehemwah shouted.

"Damn, girl," Lydia 2's voice responded in Lydia Ehemwah's ear. "What do you want?"

"Get your butt up here and help me do this inventory, that's what!" Lydia Ehemwah barked before shutting off her internal comm by tapping her left wrist with her right index finger. She turned to Lydia 3, who was standing behind her, and said, "I don't know what that wench's problem is sometimes."

"You know she likes to be defiant," Lydia 3 offered. "She likes to do her own thing."

"You mean prove that she's her own woman?" Lydia Ehemwah said. "That's a joke. She's not her own woman—she's me, just like you are. We're all the same woman." The two women were physically identical, each having a thin muscular frame, sable-brown skin, tightly coiled black hair in a close-cropped trim, dark brown eyes with long lashes, a soft nose with a broad bridge, and a wide mouth with plump lips. The utilitarian, pocket-covered jumpsuits they wore differed only in color, Lydia Ehemwah's red versus Lydia 3's tan.

Lydia 2 climbed a ladder to the storage room, joining Lydia Ehemwah and Lydia 3. The elder of the two clones, Lydia 2 wore a black jumpsuit and a different hairstyle from her clone sister Lydia 3 and her original Lydia Ehemwah, long braids pulled back with a band into a loose ponytail that hung down her back.

"About time you decided to join us," Lydia Ehemwah said to Lydia 2.

"Whatever," Lydia 2 snapped. "I'm here now. I'm ready to work. You don't have to give me a bunch of shit."

"I wouldn't give you shit if you were here on time," Lydia Ehemwah said, and then she handed Lydia 2 a pair of translucent gloves with a metallic sheen. After handing another pair of these gloves to Lydia 3 and putting on a pair herself, she declared, "Let's start counting and adding, ladies."

After finishing the inventory, the three women sat in the spaceship's small community room to eat dinner from their supply of pre-made instant meals. Sitting on separate, cushioned seats with trays in their laps, the women chatted. They were able to relax as the ship was on autopilot in an orbit around the gas giant from which they finished drawing and storing the materials they had inventoried.

"We got a big haul of jump juice this time, huh, Lydia E?" Lydia 3 said.

"Yep, and a good amount of light gas," Lydia Ehemwah replied. "Light gas" and "jump juice" were common slang terms for the two forms of fuel that made interplanetary and interstellar travel possible. "That's 50,000,000 credits worth once we deliver."

"Whew!" Lydia 2 exclaimed. "Let's take a break and jump off to that resort on Pele-Mahuika. I could use a volcanic mud bath." She sat back on her seat and raised her arms in a slow stretch as she added, "Oh yeah, a night-time bath in the mud pool with Mt. Keezheekoni lighting up the whole place with its eruptions and lava flows— mmph!"

"I like the fizzy water soaks myself," Lydia 3 chimed in. "That soda pool with the geyser next to it just makes me tingle." She feigned a shiver and giggled.

"We're not going there," Lydia Ehemwah said.

"Why?" asked Lydia 2, putting her arms down and glaring at her original. "It's not like we can't afford it!"

"That's got nothing to do with it," Lydia Ehemwah said. "I've got over 500 million credits stored up. That's more than enough for me to quit this business and jump back home."

Lydia 2 and Lydia 3 stopped eating and looked at their original. "What do you mean *jump back home*?" Lydia 2 asked. "We're already home."

"I mean back to Earth," Lydia Ehemwah responded.

"We're gonna jump back to Earth?" Lydia 3 asked. As the ship was in another star system, travel to Earth meant engaging the jump drive that would bend space-time to take them back to the edge of the Solar System instantly, where they would, as required by safety regulations, switch to the light drive to travel at light speed or slower to get to Earth.

"After all these years?" Lydia 2 said with a rise in her voice. "Why do you want to go back to Earth?"

"Because I have enough credits to quit working and go back, that's why!" Lydia Ehemwah told her clones. "When people get rich enough so they don't have to work, they quit working and settle down, just like Mama did."

"That doesn't mean we have to jump back to Earth," Lydia 2 said. "We can settle down somewhere else."

"I don't want to live on one of the colonies," Lydia Ehemwah responded. "I want to breathe natural air and feel open space. Those big domes on the colonies are just as confining as a spaceship."

"I wasn't talking about the colonies!" Lydia 2 said. "I don't want to live anywhere under Earth jurisdiction."

"There's no difference between living on an Earther colony and somewhere else," Lydia Ehemwah said. "There's no other known planet where Earthers can live without being enclosed in artificial environments but Earth. Besides, it's *home*. We were born there and raised there. You need to be glad for that." Most "Earthers" lived on planets outside the Solar System, with only Earth-born people allowed to live on the planet of origin permanently.

"I don't care about none of that!" Lydia 2 shouted and, tossing her tray aside, stood up and left the room.

After a moment, Lydia Ehemwah said, "What is wrong with her?"

"I don't know," Lydia 3 said. "I'll go talk to her." She rose from her seat, walked to where Lydia 2 had been sitting, and picked up her tray from the floor. After placing both Lydia 2's tray and hers into a receptacle, she went to Lydia 2's sleep chamber, where she knew her clone sister would be.

The spherical chamber's rough-textured, dull metallic walls were adorned only with a large round window, directly opposite the chamber doorway, that showed the expanse of space outside. Lydia 2 sat on the sleep pad that made up the room's floor; her arms were wrapped around her knees, and she faced the window.

Lydia 2's back was to Lydia 3 as she stood in the chamber doorway. "Lydia?" Lydia 3 gently called to her clone sister.

"She doesn't care about us," Lydia 2 sobbed. She sniffed and snorted, letting Lydia 3 know that she was crying.

"What do you mean?" Lydia 3 asked as she stepped onto the sleep pad, got on her knees and crawled over to Lydia 2.

"She...doesn't give a damn about us!" Lydia 2 said, choking on her words as she cried.

"Please," Lydia 3 said, sitting next to Lydia 2 and placing a hand on her back. "Talk to me. Tell me why you're so upset over Lydia wanting to go back to Earth."

Lydia 2 lifted her head and turned to Lydia 3. "What is wrong with you? If you don't recognize why going back to Earth is the last thing I or you should want, then I don't have anything to say to you."

Lydia 3 was hurt and confused by this, but she persisted in trying to both comfort and question Lydia 2. "Why do you have to be like that? Please, you shouldn't be mad at me when I'm here trying to listen and understand you."

Lydia 2 clicked her tongue, rolled her eyes, and then said, "You must like being treated like dirt."

"Uh, no I don't," Lydia 3 responded tentatively.

"No, you *must*," Lydia 2 said more forcefully. "Because that's how we're going to be treated back on Earth!" With that, Lydia 2 rose up onto her hands and knees and crawled along the soft pad to the window. As she gazed through the glass at the stars outside, she said, "After all the times we've visited Earther colonies—you know how we're treated, how we have to act, how it is in those places for us!"

"I know," Lydia 3 said. "It's hard for us when we haven't lived in Earther jurisdiction for so long—we just visit those places every now and then—but we've been fortunate. We've had a life of travel and freedom that most people like us don't have. And Lydia has never treated us as lower than or less than she is. She's our big sister; she loves us..."

"She's our original," Lydia 2 interrupted. "She's over us, she gets to tell us we've got to go live on Earth for the rest of our lives, and we can't do anything about it—big sister, my ass!"

"Lydia, she owns this ship, and it's her business," Lydia 3 said. "If she wants to stop working and go back to Earth, she can do that."

"She can do that because she's an original and we're clones!" Lydia 2 turned away from the window and yelled at Lydia 3. "She owns this ship and this business because we are not allowed to own *anything!*"

Lydia 3 backed away from Lydia 2; she was at a loss for what to say. She had witnessed a lifetime of seeing Lydia 2 rage against any assertion of Lydia Ehemwah's rank of "big sister"; she had seen Lydia 2 whine and pout every time they went to an Earther colony. On those visits, Lydia 2 would never leave the ship.

4

Lydia 3 liked the life of resource prospecting and trading that the three have lived for the past two decades: searching for and harvesting various metals, liquids, gasses and other forms of matter on various planets, moons and asteroids and trading them for other resources or selling them for credits. The most important and enriching materials they retrieved, traded and sold were the light gas for light- and sub-light speed travel within a star-planetary system and the rarer jump juice that enabled "jumps" from one star system to another.

Lydia Ehemwah had inherited the business and the starship from her mother, who quit working to jump back to Earth and start the family that consisted of her daughter and her daughter's clones. Once the Lydias took on the business they found it to be a rough and wild life: The ship was devoted more to creating a safe space for storing massive amounts of often-volatile cargo and powering safe and speedy travel than for modern comfort for the crew. The work of acquiring materials from often uninhabited and hostile environments could be dangerous.

However, it was also a lucrative livelihood that afforded them liberty to indulge in the variety of sights and experiences that interplanetary travel allowed. Spa-style treatments amid natural wonders on Pele-Mahuika's resorts weren't the only sensual delights the three women had enjoyed in their travels: They had tasted exotic foods, sampled mind-altering substances, and experimented with a variety of activities, some considered illicit in Earther communities.

It was a great lifestyle, but none of the women were getting any younger, Lydia 3 thought—it would be nice to settle down somewhere great while they were all still young enough to enjoy the riches from their business. And Earth was still the planet of beauty and full freedom for Earthers—life without artificial supports, a low human population, the vast majority of the planet—known as the Outlands, in contrast to the urban meglopolises—given over to nature in all its splendor.

As Earth-borns, they had a right to this paradise that few humans had. For Lydia 3, going back to Earth now was a good idea. As for the social environment, she could live with it—it's what they grew up with; she lived with it again every time she left the ship with Lydia Ehemwah on visits to Earther colonies, and she was fine with it. She was a clone; she recognized and accepted her place in Earther society.

Knowing all this, Lydia 3 couldn't figure out a way to make Lydia 2 feel better about the situation. Lydia 3 could only say to her clone sister, "Lydia, I know you don't like being in Earther-controlled places, but Earth is such a wonderful world. Don't you remember that? If you want, we can travel a lot to the Outlands so you don't have to spend a lot of time in the city. I know and you know Lydia would be fine with that."

Lydia 2 turned her back on Lydia 3 to look out the window. "I shouldn't have to have Lydia's approval to do a damn thing. Now leave me alone."

Lydia 3 brushed back tears from her eyes before she stood up and left the chamber.

Lydia 3 found Lydia Ehemwah in the community room stretched out on one of the seats, watching a holo-video of a parrot-inhabited forest in Australia. The three of them enjoyed viewing the 3-D projections of Earth's wonders more than any other kinds of holo-videos, and they had thousands of these videos stored in their computer.

"Australia has the greatest diversity of parrot species on Earth," Lydia Ehemwah said. "They come in so many colors. They make New Guinea birds of paradise look dull. It will be nice to see them."

"Yeah," Lydia 3 agreed, and she sat down next to her original. "We can go outside the cities and spend a lot of time in the Outlands with the credits we have now."

"Uh-huh," Lydia Ehemwah responded. "We sure couldn't do that before. Mama always wished she had enough credits to take us on more than one trip a year."

"Yeah." Lydia 3 sighed. It was hard for her to think about Mama without feeling sad.

"We can have a fun and relaxing life back on Earth," Lydia Ehemwah continued. "We don't have to work, and we can travel as much as we want. I don't get why Lydia is losing her mind over going back."

"You know she doesn't like being around Earthers," Lydia 3 said.

"She doesn't like being treated like a clone," Lydia Ehemwah added. "Mama raised us together to be sisters, and everything I had, you both had. Most clones don't get treated like that."

"I know," Lydia 3 said.

"Then as soon as we grew up, we left home and started working in this business," Lydia Ehemwah continued. "We've spent most of our lives being away from Earther society. In a lot of ways, she's gotten spoiled. She's had the privilege to not act like she's a clone. But she is; she's my sister, but she is my clone. She belongs to me; she *is* me. You both are my flesh and blood. I've always treated you two as good as I treat myself. That's how Mama raised us, and that's not going to change when we jump back to Earth."

"You should go tell her that," Lydia 3 said.

"She already knows all that," Lydia Ehemwah said. "Again, she doesn't want to be treated like a clone, and I can't control what other Earthers say or do. If she wants to just never leave our home except when we go to the Outlands, that's fine. But we're jumping back home so we can live and breathe on a planet we were born to live on."

"Please talk to Lydia," Lydia 3 insisted. "She thinks you don't care about her."

"Did she say that?" Lydia Ehemwah said, turning her head quickly to glare at Lydia.

"Yeah," said Lydia 3. "She said you don't care about us."

"I love her!" Lydia Ehemwah spat out. "And she says I don't care about her? She doesn't know how good she has it, how good her life is because she's my clone!" Lydia Ehemwah stood up. "I was going to just let her have her little pouting spell and just leave her alone, like I always do, but you know what? You're right—I am going to talk to her. We're going to have this out right now." Lydia Ehemwah started to walk out of the room. When Lydia 3 started to rise up, Lydia Ehemwah said, "Uh-uh, don't follow me. This is between her and me. I don't need you trying to mediate or hold us back. It's all coming out, and let the chips fall where they may!"

As Lydia Ehemwah left the room, Lydia 3 turned to the holo-video and watched red-tailed black cockatoo pairs feed and groom each other as they perched on a tree branch.

"Lydia! Lydia!" A harsh, choked-up voice in her ear startled Lydia 3 out of her engrossment with the holo-video.

"What's going on? You all right?" Lydia 3 answered, knowing from a lifetime of listening that it was Lydia 2 speaking through her comm.

"Come here, right now!" Lydia 2 shouted.

Lydia 3 got up and hurried to Lydia 2's chamber. She stopped at the entrance, frozen with shock at what she saw: Lydia Ehemwah was lying on the sleep pad, motionless. A large blood pool was under her head. Lydia 2 was kneeling over Lydia Ehemwah, holding her original's head in her hands.

"Lydia!" Lydia 3 screamed. "What happened? Oh, never mind what happened," she changed her thinking from panic to action. "I'm going to get the medikit."

"Don't bother," Lydia 2 said with a soft sob.

"What do you mean, 'Don't bother'?" Lydia 3 shouted. "Lydia's hurt!"

"She's more than hurt!" Lydia 2 shouted back. "*She's dead!*"

Lydia 3 was stunned into silence for a moment. "You don't know that! She could be unconscious! Or in a coma!"

"I know she's dead!" Lydia 2 screamed.

"You—don't—know—shit!" Lydia 3 shouted, then she left to retrieve the medikit.

When Lydia 3 returned to the chamber, Lydia 2 was still on her knees, holding Lydia Ehemwah's head. Lydia 2 stepped into the room and walked to her clone sister and her original, making sure to step carefully on the cushioned floor. Once she reached the two women, she set down the medikit and sat down on her knees next to Lydia 2.

"I need you to move," she said to Lydia 2 quietly.

Lydia 2 stayed where she was.

"Move, damnit!" Lydia 3 ordered and then pushed her clone sister, making Lydia 2 fall to the side. Lydia 3 then opened the medikit case and retrieved sensors that she planted on Lydia Ehemwah's forehead and heart. Then she placed a mask-like device over her original's nose and mouth.

After activating the medikit's bioscanner with a touch on the case, Lydia 3 read the results on the case's screen: "No heartbeat...no respiration...no brain waves...brain irreparably damaged by trauma...no resuscitation or revival possible."

Upon hearing Lydia 3 read the bioscanner's results, Lydia 2 slowly sat up on her knees again and reached for Lydia 3. "I told you. She's dead."

As Lydia 2 placed her hands on Lydia 3's shoulders, Lydia 3 said, "Why? How?" She turned to Lydia 2 and demanded with a rising voice, "How did her brain get 'irreparably damaged by trauma'? How, Lydia!"

"She was going off at me!" Lydia 2 answered loudly, and then with a softer voice added, "Talking about how I'm ungrateful and spoiled and how I act like I'm not a clone and all this other mess. She yelled all that in my face, and then she started pushing me, and I pushed back, and we started fighting, and she hit her head!"

"Where?" Lydia 3 asked, holding back the flood of grief that threatened to drown her. "Where did she hit her head so she 'irreparably damaged' her brain?"

"Right there," Lydia 2 said, pointing at a blood spot low on the wall, near the window.

Lydia 3 crawled over to the wall and stared at the spot. A loud, hard sob forced its way out of Lydia 3's throat, and with that the flood of grief finally broke through. Wailing, choking, she beat the wall near the spot with her fist, pounding it over and over again.

Lydia 2 moved behind Lydia 3 and wrapped her arms around her, grabbing Lydia 3's fist and pulling her away from the wall. Holding Lydia 3 tightly, Lydia 2 rocked her clone sister as she howled and wept.

After a while, Lydia 3's crying left her exhausted, breathless and limp. Lydia 2 rose up on her feet, pulling Lydia 3 up with her. "Come on. Let me take you to your room. It's almost sleep shift anyway," Lydia 2 quietly urged her clone sister. With Lydia 3 leaning on Lydia 2, the clone sisters left the chamber.

Lydia 2 led her clone sister to lie down on the cushioned floor of her sleep chamber. As Lydia 3 lay curled up and sniffling, Lydia 2 sat next to her and stroked Lydia 3's forehead.

"Go to sleep now," Lydia 2 said. "We can take care of Lydia when the sleep shift is over. Chamber! Lights off!" she commanded the chamber's controls, and the room went dark.

Despite the shock and pain she suffered from, Lydia 3's exhaustion forced her to fall asleep.

Lydia 3 woke up to the sight of Lydia 2 sitting with her back against the wall, her arms wrapped around her knees, staring at Lydia 3.

"We've got to go take care of Lydia now," Lydia 2 said flatly.

The rush of memory threatened to engulf Lydia 3 with grief again. When Lydia 3 gasped and sobbed, Lydia 2 quickly hushed her: "Shush! Don't start crying again. Not now. We've got to move her." Lydia 2 crawled across the cushion and thrust her face directly in front of Lydia 3's, her eyes boring into her clone sister's. "I don't want to do it, either. I don't want to go in there, either. But we have to, all right?"

Tears continued to run down her face, but Lydia 3 nodded in agreement.

Lydia 2 stood up and helped her clone sister up. They left Lydia 3's sleep chamber and went back to Lydia 2's chamber.

The clone sisters stood at the entrance and looked into the room at the body of their original. After a pause, Lydia 2 said, "I just thought—I'm going to go get one of her wraps from her room."

"Why?" Lydia 3 asked weakly. Lydia Ehemwah's full-body shawl-like wraps were her favorite garments to relax and sleep in after a full work shift.

"A wrap will be big enough to cover her up with, and it'll make her easier to carry," Lydia 2 answered matter-of-factly as she left, sounding as if her clone sister had asked her for direction on how to operate a piece of equipment.

Lydia 3 looked down at Lydia Ehemwah's body, but she didn't enter the chamber. She felt she couldn't go in without her clone sister—she couldn't come near her original without feeling the pain and falling apart all over again.

Holding a shimmering blue wrap balled up in her arms, Lydia 2 came back to the chamber entrance and stepped past her clone sister to go inside. She set the wrap down away from Lydia Ehemwah's body and then sat on her knees next to it. Then she started removing the medical sensors and respirator mask from the body and placing them in the medikit.

"Here, come get this," Lydia 2 told her sister, pointing at the medikit.

Lydia 3 swallowed hard, and then she stepped into the room. When she picked up the medikit, Lydia 2 said, "Take it out of the room, then come back and help me."

Struggling not to think about their original lying on the floor, Lydia 3 quickly left the room to put the medikit back in its storage place. When she came back, Lydia 2 had spread the wrap on the floor so it lay in a big blue square next to Lydia Ehemwah's body.

"Come help me roll her up in this," Lydia 2 said as she knelt next to the body on the side opposite from where the wrap was spread. Lydia 3 stepped over to her clone sister and knelt next to her. Lydia 2 slid her hands under the body; following her clone sister's lead, Lydia 3 did the same. Together, they lifted one side of the body and rolled it onto its side. They then pushed it over farther until it lay on its front, covering one edge of the wrap.

"Here, grab the wrap with one hand and kind of pull it up while we roll her again," Lydia 2 said. "That way, we can wrap this around her as we roll her."

Lydia 2 did as her clone sister said, and they both rolled the body another turn while making sure the wrap covered it. As a result, the front of the body was completely covered by the edge of the sheet.

"Now, we can just keep rolling and rolling until she's wrapped up," Lydia 2 said.

The clone sisters finished rolling the body, leaving it completely enshrouded in the wrap.

"Now you grab that end," Lydia 2 said, pointing at the end of the wrap that covered the feet. Lydia 3 stood up and grasped the wrap, cinching the end with both hands.

After Lydia 2 did the same, she said, "All right, on the count of three, we're going to pick her up. One, two, three!" The clone sisters hoisted the dead weight of their original, struggling to raise the body waist-high. "Come on, come on, let's move her to the zero storage room now, before we drop her!" Lydia 2 grunted.

The zero-degree storage chamber was one of the ship's rooms for storing commodities that had to be kept at certain temperatures. After the women placed the body into the chamber, Lydia 3 broke down again, sinking to the floor at the chamber door. Lydia 2 bent down to help her clone sister up.

"Come on, let's go to the community room. Come on, get up," Lydia 2 urged, pulling Lydia 3 up then holding her with one arm around her waist as they walked to the room.

Lydia 2 guided Lydia 3 to a seat and then took another seat directly across from her. After watching Lydia 3 weep with her face in her hands, Lydia 2 said, "Lydia, I'm upset and hurt just like you. But we both can't be falling apart right now. You need to listen to me."

Lydia 3 still wept and covered her face in her hands. Lydia 2 stood up, grabbed her seat, and moved it to place it next to Lydia 3. Then she sat down and took her clone sister's hands.

"Look at me. Now!" Lydia 2 hissed, pulling at Lydia 3's hands.

Lydia 3 allowed Lydia 2 to lower her hands from her face and hold them. Lydia 3 looked up at her clone sister with wet, red eyes. Lydia 2's eyes were dry, wide and sharp.

"Now, listen," Lydia 2 began. "We could take Lydia to the nearest Earther colony, but we should jump back to Earth because that's what she wanted."

That sounded right and reasonable to Lydia 3. "All right," she agreed.

"But there's one problem with taking her to Earth," Lydia 2 added. She waited for Lydia 3 to respond, but her clone sister was too weary from grief to react.

Lydia 2 continued, "If we take her to Earth, or to any Earther-controlled area, they'll take the ship from us. They'll take the inventory from us. They'll take the credits from us. They'll take everything and give it all to our nearest genetic relation. That includes *us*."

She paused again to get Lydia 3's reaction. Lydia 3 sniffled a little but still said nothing.

"Lydia!" Lydia 2 said with a rough voice. "Don't you know what that means for us?"

Her clone sister's harsh, desperate tone shook Lydia 3 out of her numb grief but left her bewildered. "I—don't—understand," Lydia 3 slowly, softly responded.

"Damnit!" Lydia 2 snapped, dropping Lydia 3's hands and sitting back on her seat. "Like I said, you must like being treated like dirt." She pushed a breath out of her mouth with a harsh huff and then said, "We clones *can't own anything*, remember? And we have to be in the custody of an original. So guess what? We jump to Earth, we get everything taken from us, and then they give us to one of Lydia's cousins or nieces or nephews, or whoever the hell is her closest relative. It doesn't matter because we'll have nothing, we'll be stuck in Earther jurisdiction, and we'll be *treated like dirt!*"

Lydia 2's anger and fear was too much for Lydia 3 to comprehend on top of the death of her original. Lydia 3 stared at her clone sister, overwhelmed and unable to speak.

Lydia 2 had stopped looking at her clone sister; she sat back on the seat with her arms crossed and her eyes rolled back. "You know," she said with slow deliberation, "We could just never go to an Earther-controlled place again, keep the ship and the credits, have her body processed, and then scatter her on a desert planet or moon."

The suggestion knocked Lydia 3 out of her confusion and grief and into a rage. "Are you crazy?" she yelled. "We are not abandoning her on some rock somewhere! Have you lost your damn mind!" Lydia 3 leapt out of her seat and grabbed Lydia 2 by her jumpsuit.

"Hey! Get off me! Let me go!" Lydia 2 yelled, grabbing her clone sister's arms and trying to pull them away.

"We're taking Lydia to Earth! You hear me!" Lydia 3 yelled, shaking Lydia 2 until she almost fell out of her seat. "I don't ever want to hear you talking about dumping her on some rock again!"

"All right, all right!" Lydia 2 said. "We're taking her to Earth! Now let me go!" Lydia 3 released her grip on Lydia 2. "Damn! What's wrong with you?" Lydia 2 said, straightening her clothing.

"What's wrong with you?" Lydia 3 snapped at her. "You're the one talking that shit about dumping our big sister on a damn rock!" Lydia 3's rage was barely restrained and ready to pounce on her clone sister again.

"All right," Lydia 2 said, lowering her voice. "I'm sorry I said that. But I was just trying to say that we could avoid going to any Earther-controlled places because if we did, we could keep everything that you and I and Lydia spent all these years earning. We don't have to lose everything and become some Earther's property."

Lydia 3 still stood over her clone sister, her face tight with rage and confusion. Lydia 2 took Lydia 3's hand and said, "Please, sit down and just listen to me, all right? Like I said, we're taking Lydia to Earth." Lydia 2 squeezed her clone sister's hand and looked at her with wide eyes.

After taking a deep sigh, Lydia 3 sat down and crossed her arms, looking at her clone sister with a cocked head and a tired gaze.

Placing her hand on Lydia 3's knee, Lydia 2 said, "I've been thinking: There is a way we can take Lydia back to Earth and not have to lose everything." She stopped speaking to check Lydia 3's reaction. Her clone sister was still looking at her, still looking weary, still sitting, still not enraged.

Lydia 2 continued, "When we get to Earth, we can tell the authorities there that Lydia is a clone." Again, she stopped to see what Lydia 3 would say or do.

Straightening her tilted head to look with a wrinkled brow at Lydia 2, Lydia 3 said, "Why would we want to do that?"

Taking a breath of relief at Lydia 3's relatively calm reaction, Lydia 2 explained, "If they believe Lydia is a clone and one of us is an original, then we can keep everything and live how we want without a custodian."

Lydia 3 dropped her arms, placing her hands on her knees, and sat up slowly to lean toward Lydia 2. Her lips parted, but her mouth said nothing. After a few seconds, Lydia 3 finally said, making each word an exclamation, "Are—you—crazy? Have—you—lost—your—damn—mind?"

Mocking her clone sister, Lydia 2 said just as slowly and loudly, "No—I—haven't—lost—my—mind! What I don't want to lose is my life!" Lydia 2 shook her head and held up her hands, shaking and pushing at the air as if she were shoving away Lydia 3's protests. Then she took a breath and placed her hands in her lap, clasping them tightly. Lydia 2 looked up at her clone sister with eyes that were wide and wet with the beginnings of tears.

Lydia 3, moved by what she saw as her clone sister's show of grief and pain, relented in attacking Lydia 2 for her idea. However, Lydia 3 still felt the need to address Lydia 2's proposal. "To pass Lydia off as a clone, we would have to get past the eye scan and the hand scan," Lydia 3 said, "and you know that's impossible."

"It's not impossible. We can beat them," Lydia 2 quickly responded.

"How the hell can we beat the scans?" Lydia 3 said. "We'll get scanned as soon as we set foot in Earther jurisdiction."

"We can beat the scans," Lydia 2 insisted. "You forget that we've got over 500 million credits, and Pele-Mahuika doesn't just have volcanic mud baths and mineral baths for sale. They also have cosmetic procedures. They can change, or transplant, anything."

Comprehension slowly came to Lydia 3, and with it she sat back in her seat and stared hard at Lydia 2. "You want to transplant Lydia's eyes and hands," Lydia 3 said, "into one of *us*?"

"We'd just need the flesh off her palms and fingers," Lydia 2 bluntly clarified. "And I'll take the transplant of that and her eyes. It's my idea, so I'll take that on."

Lydia 3 swallowed hard and then shook her head hard. "Lydia, our big sister—she's—gone," Lydia 3 forced out of herself, "and you're talking about having her eyes cut out and her hands skinned for you to wear like a new suit!"

"It's either that, or we lose everything and get placed in the custody of people we don't even know!" Lydia 2 shouted. "No credits, no ship, no freedom, no life! Do you really want that?" Lydia 2 reached and took Lydia 3's face in her hands. Her face only millimeters away from her clone sister, Lydia 2 looked into Lydia 3's eyes and asked, "Do you? Do you really want that to happen?"

Lydia 3 swallowed hard, took a breath, and then said, "I don't know. I just can't think about it right now."

Lydia 2 let go of her clone sister's face and sat back in the chair, crossing her arms.

"I can't think at all," Lydia 3 said. "I mean, damnit, Lydia is dead!" She covered her hands with her face and started weeping.

Arms still crossed, Lydia 2 looked away from her clone sister. Lydia 2's eyes had a stare that seemed to gaze at a faraway place that no one but her could see. "Yes, Lydia is dead, and our lives as we know it could end with hers. We might as well be dead with her. *I* might as well be dead," she declared; then she stood up and walked out of the chamber, leaving Lydia 3 to continue to weep alone.

A short time later, Lydia 2 called to Lydia 3's comm, "Lydia, come to the zero storage room." Lydia 3 sat up quickly, startled and puzzled by the call. Despite her confusion, she got up and left the chamber.

The door to the zero-degree storage chamber was closed. Just when Lydia 3 approached it, Lydia 2 called out over the comm, "I'm in the chamber, but don't open the door! Stand there and listen.

"I have a hypo-pen filled with 100 cc's of Dormirex, and I'm holding it at my neck, at my one of the big blood vessels there," Lydia

2 continued, her voice steady. "Losing everything we have and going back to Earth is as good as being dead to me, so I figure I might as well die."

"No!" Lydia 3 screamed, panic surging through her body and threatening to explode in her mind. She grabbed the door handle of the zero-degree storage chamber and pulled it open.

"Stay right where you are or I'll use it *right now!*" Lydia 2 shouted. She lay on a table next to the covered body of Lydia Ehemwah, holding the slim hypo-pen against her throat.

"Please, please, don't," Lydia 3 plead from the doorway.

"I figured I'd save you the trouble of having to put my body into the zero storage room," Lydia 2 said matter-of-factly, her words pushing clouds of visible cold breath out of her mouth. "I could have just did it and not told you, and let you just find me in here. But I wanted you to know that I'm for real when I say I'd rather be dead than have nothing and be nobody back on Earth!"

The idea of having two dead sisters in less than 24 Earth hours drove itself like a spike through Lydia 3's head and made her sink to her knees. "Please, please, don't do it," Lydia 3 continued to beg as she choked back sobs.

"You want to jump back to Earth and lose everything, fine. You fire up the jump drive and go," Lydia 2 said. "But that doesn't mean I have to. Just make sure we both get disposed of together," she added, placing her free hand on the wrap that held her dead original. "Tell your custodian that Lydia wanted our remains to be scattered in the Outlands."

"Damnit, don't!" Lydia 3 screamed. "Pleeese!" She wrapped her arms around her body and rocked on her knees. "I love you. Please don't die. Don't leave me alone. I couldn't take it."

"You say you love me, but you don't care about how I feel," Lydia 2 said. "You've known all this time that I don't want to live in Earther jurisdiction, and you know why. Now you want us to lose everything along with Lydia, and I tell you we don't have to do that, but you don't care!"

"I never said that!" Lydia 3 insisted. "I just couldn't think! You're telling me all this stuff when all I can think about is Lydia being—gone! It's just too much!"

"Losing everything and going back to Earth to be in somebody's custody is too much for me!" Lydia yelled back. "I'm ready to die over it. I'm ready to be cold and dead just like Lydia!"

"No!" Lydia 3 shouted. "I didn't say no to what you want to do. It's just too much for me to think about. But I don't want you to die. If your doing what you want to do—the transplant thing—means you don't die, then go ahead and do it. I just don't want you to die. Please, please don't die." Hard sobs stopped Lydia 3 from being able to plead any longer.

Lydia 2 sat up and slid off the table onto her feet. She walked slowly toward her sister, shivering from the chill in the chamber, still holding the hypo-pen in one hand. Once she stood in front of Lydia 3, she bent down to sit on her knees. Taking Lydia 3's right hand in hers, Lydia 2 turned up Lydia 3's palm and placed the hypo-pen in it. "Here," Lydia 2 said.

Lydia 3 tossed the hypo-pen against a wall, and then she wrapped her arms tightly around Lydia 2. As Lydia 3 cried loudly into her clone sister's shoulder, Lydia 2 held her and shed tears as well, but Lydia 2 was silent.

This excerpt was published (in slightly different form) in *Jalada 02: Afrofuture(s)*, January 15, 2015.

https://jaladaafrica.org/2015/01/15/secret-insurrection-by-stephani-maari-booker/

Secret Insurrection:
Blood Bonds, Memory Binds

A private commodities trading ship was docked at one of the massive artificial islands, anchored in Earth's oceans, constructed as small space vessel and large aircraft ports. Before landing, the ship had notified the Terrestrial Port Authority of its arrival and the death of a crew member, the senior of one of the ship owner's two clones.

The two remaining crew members—after being positively identified by retinal/iris and hand-print scans as owner Lydia Ehemwah and her second clone, Lydia 3—stood aside as TPA officials boarded their ship The officials retrieved the body from the ship's zero-degree storage chamber, placing it in a sterile preserving casket before removing it from the ship to be sent to the nearest Thantoservice Center to be processed for disposal. As the clone's original reported her death as being caused by an accidental fall, the TPA officials did not visually record the scene where the death occurred nor did they send the body to an autopsy scan, as would be standard for a death of an original by any causes other than advanced aging. Less than 12 hours later, the TPA notified the owner of the ship that the official processing was completed and that she was free to leave the port with her surviving clone to claim the remains of her deceased clone.

An air shuttle landed on a pad at the top of a 650-meter skyscraper, one of the many that made up Michiganopolis, the mega-city that surrounded the southern shore of Lake Michigan. The Lydias were two of the passengers who disembarked and took elevators to their apartment homes in the slim, silver tower. Eventually, the Lydias arrived at the 150th floor and walked to their new home.

The two women were silent with each other throughout the short journey from the port to the Thantoservice Center and then to the skyscraper; they didn't exchange a word until after entering the apartment.

"Ahhhhh!" Lydia 3 loudly sighed as the door closed, and she turned to hug Lydia 2 tightly.

Lydia 2 wrapped one arm around her clone sister; the other arm held a white box that contained their original's remains. "You did good," she said quietly. "You didn't say much, and you cried a lot. That's what they would expect from a clone whose sister is dead."

"And you didn't cry at all," Lydia 3 said, pulling back a little to look Lydia 2 in the face. "How could you hold back and be so calm through all this?"

"Originals don't view clone deaths as a big deal," Lydia 2 said. "I couldn't be carrying on crying like you when I'm supposed to be an original. As far as anybody else is concerned, I could just go order a clone baby to replace Lydia and move on."

"Damn, that's so cold!" Lydia 3 let go of her clone sister and backed away.

"I'm just saying that's the way they think here," Lydia 2 said. "You know that. Besides, as an original, I had to have myself together to get us past the port authority and get us here."

"You're not an original," Lydia 3 corrected.

"That's what I'm supposed to be, right?" Lydia 2 shouted. "That's what I have to be from now on!"

Lydia 3 stared back at her clone; then she dropped her head as the memories rushed through her mind: *Lydia! What happened? Oh, never mind what happened. I'm going to get the medikit."*

"Don't bother."

"What do you mean, 'Don't bother'? Lydia's hurt!"

"She's more than hurt! She's dead!"

"Look, you were fine with Lydia taking us back to Earth, so now we're here," Lydia 2 said. "As long as I don't have to live as a clone anymore, I'm fine with staying here; but we can always just go scatter Lydia's remains in the Outlands and then just hop back on the ship and keep on traveling. What do you want to do?"

Lydia 3 shook her head slowly.

"We clones can't own anything, remember? And we have to be in the custody of an original. So guess what? We go to Earth, we get everything taken from us, and then they give us to one of Lydia's cousins or nieces or nephews, or whoever the hell is her closest relative. It doesn't matter because we'll have nothing, we'll be stuck in Earther jurisdiction, and we'll be treated like dirt!"

20

Lydia 2 took a step and placed her free hand on her clone sister's shoulder. "Look, we don't have to decide or do anything right now. We have a lot of freedom now, and a whole lot of credits on top of that to do whatever we want. Why don't we just get something to eat, sit down, and watch some 'net? We can just stay in and then go to the Outlands whenever we get ready."

"I just want to go lie down," Lydia 3 whispered.

"There is a way we can take Lydia back to Earth and not have to lose everything."

"Okay, but at least let me get us both something to eat, all right?" Lydia 2 said, walking into the main room. She touched a spot on a bare-looking gray wall, and a drawer opened up. She placed the box with her original's remains inside. After touching the front of the drawer, the drawer disappeared in the wall.

"To pass Lydia off as a clone, we would have to get past the eye scan and the hand scan, and you know that's impossible."

"We can beat the scans. You forget that we've got over 500 million credits, and Pele-Mahuika doesn't just have volcanic mud baths and mineral baths for sale. They also have cosmetic procedures. They can change, or transplant, anything."

"You want to transplant Lydia's eyes and hands...into one of us?"

Choking on a sob, Lydia 3 rushed to a bedroom and closed the door.

After a few days spent in the apartment, the Lydias took another air shuttle to the regional air/space port island. The shuttle had 12 rows of four seats divided by an aisle that placed two seats on one side and two on the other. The shuttle was a little less than half full, so the two women had a fair choice of seats.

There was a mixture of originals and clones aboard the shuttle. They were easy to tell apart: Originals dressed as individuals, wearing everything from slacks and plain shirts to short skirts, to long-sleeved, ankle-length tunics, with accessories ranging from simple caps to elaborately wrapped headscarves, all in a variety of patterns and colors ranging from solid black to brassy metallics. The clones were allowed to wear only a form-fitting body suit, available in a limited assortment of solid colors but plain and un-accessorized, not even with pockets.

Lydia 3 immediately took a seat next to a window. Lydia 2 followed her clone sister to the seat next to her, but she did not sit down.

"I want this seat," Lydia 2 said quietly but firmly.

"But I want a window seat," Lydia 3 protested mildly. "Why don't you sit in the seat in front of me?" she proposed, nodding her head toward the back of that seat. "Then we'd both have window seats."

Lydia 2 hardened her voice. "Get up—now!"

Lydia 3 opened her mouth to snap back at Lydia 2, then she remembered that here in public, she wasn't needling a clone sister— she was defying an original. She closed her mouth, swallowed hard, and then stood up. The two women changed places, Lydia 2 taking the window seat and Lydia 3 sitting next to her.

Lydia 2 took Lydia 3's hand and squeezed it, almost but not quite tightly enough to hurt. As she did this, Lydia 2's eyes bore into her secret clone sister. Lydia 3 lowered her head and sat back into the seat. Lydia 2 released Lydia 3's hand and then turned her head to look out the window.

The Lydias were silent for the rest of the ride as the shuttle stopped at other skyscraper air pads to pick up more passengers. At one stop, Lydia 3 heard the pilot say, "There's only 11 seats available. Some of you will have to take the next shuttle." Then the shuttle started filling up with a crowd of people. As the passengers entered, the clones aboard started rising from their seats and moving into the aisle. Originals then took the clones' former seats.

Lydia 3 stood up and ceded her seat to a male original. As he sat down, Lydia 2 nodded to him and then resumed watching the view from the window. As the man placed a 'net-viewing visor over his eyes and sat back in his seat, Lydia 3—standing in the aisle, pressed by the bodies of other clones—stared at the sight of her clone sister wearing one of Lydia Ehemwah's body wraps, sitting with an original as all other clones stood.

Lydia 3 felt a squeezing pain in her gut. She wanted to go to the onboard lavatory to vomit, but she didn't want to jostle her way through the crowd of clones to get there.

The regional air/space port was the same one the Lydias landed at when they returned to Earth, lying 100 kilometers from the North American east coast where the mega-city Atlanticopolis was located. As they waited in a lobby to board their plane, Lydia 2 took Lydia 3's hand firmly and whispered, "Keep your damn mouth shut." Lydia 2 then reached into a large shoulder bag she was carrying and pulled out a 'net-viewing visor. "Here, sit down, put these on and enjoy yourself—quietly."

Lydia 3 boarded the plane at a separate door from Lydia 2. The only clones allowed in first class were the stewards who served the passengers. Second class, where Lydia would sit, had simple rows of seats divided by an aisle, but there were more seats per row and more rows than on a shuttle. Even with more seating, the clone passengers were crowded together, ordered by a steward to fill every seat starting with the rear row with no empty seats between passengers, leaving the rear of the section filled and the front empty.

After Lydia 3 took a seat between two other passengers, she looked around. Many of the passengers, but not all, were equipped with 'net visors to help them pass the time on the long trip with one stop in Europe, one in South Asia and then Australia.

"Australia has the greatest diversity of parrot species on Earth. They come in so many colors. They make New Guinea birds of paradise look dull. It will be nice to see them."

"Yeah. We can go outside the cities and spend a lot of time in the Outlands with the credits we have now."

"Uh-huh. We sure couldn't do that before. We can have a fun and relaxing life back on Earth. We don't have to work, and we can travel as much as we want. I don't get why Lydia is losing her mind over going back."

"You know she doesn't like being around Earthers."

"She doesn't like being treated like a clone. Mama raised us together to be sisters, and everything I had, you both had. Most clones don't get treated like that."

Hey!" A man's voice cried out from behind Lydia 3, interrupting the painful flashback. "You're bumping my knees!"

"Sorry," the man next to Lydia 3 gulped out, then he pulled his seat up.

Lydia 3 rose up and looked around so she could see who was behind her. A very thin, short, elderly woman had a 'net visor on and was as quiet and still as a sleeping baby.

Lydia 3 sighed, turned back around, sat in her seat, and pushed it back to its fully reclined position. After placing her 'net visor over her eyes and wrapping the attached ear pieces around her ears, Lydia 3 sat back and tapped one side of the visor to turn it on.

A menu appeared on the right side of her vision, listing options such as "Saved Video," "Saved Sites and Stations," "Go to…" and "Recommended Sites & Stations." A small red point of light, guided by Lydia 3's eye movements, acted as a selector for the menu options. Lydia 3 moved the light to "Saved Sites & Stations" and then blinked twice. The menu disappeared, and another took its place, listing a number of different entertainment and informational 'net sites and stations retrieved from the allotment of 'net info-storage reserved for Lydia Ehemwah.

She selected "Warrior Queen of the Sahara." Her vision was filled with a three-dimensional, photo-realistic panorama of a desert oasis with a castle in the background. Words in the foreground inquired, "Watch Warrior Queen," "Be Warrior Queen" "Be Another Character." Lydia 3 selected "Watch Warrior Queen." She didn't feel like experiencing or acting out the movie from the hero's or any character's point of view, affecting the movie's actions and outcomes.

With her selection, the movie began and she was inside an ancient castle as an invisible being watching the birth of the baby who would grow up to be the great Queen Zenobia.

When the plane landed at the air/space port offshore from Europe's mega-city Britannia-Francopolis, Lydia 3 was able to grab a window seat in the exchange of passengers leaving and entering. The stop at the air/space port lasted for a few hours, and Lydia 3 took a break from watching 'net to look out a window and see the busy goings-on outside.

As she watched the landings and takeoffs of planes, shuttles and spacecrafts and people and cargo riding trams on the tarmac, Lydia 3 remembered the one other time she had ridden a plane on Earth when all three Lydias were teenagers. That trip took the Lydias and their mother first to the Europe air-space port, where they took an air shuttle to the Straits of Gibraltar. They then entered the Saharan Outlands at the North African town of Tanjah. This was the closest the four could come to the sub-Saharan home of their ancient ancestors, who long ago had immigrated from a land on the west coast of Africa to North America. The sub-Sahara was accessible only through expensive overland rides for hire across days of desert and the thick rainforest, depopulated for generations and by law inhabited only by Outland caretakers and rare visitors.

Going to Africa was a lifelong dream of the Lydias' mother, and as she and the Lydias rode through the old city center of Tanjah in a cart hitched to a mule driven by a caretaker, she mused, "At last, we're in our homeland."

"I don't live here," Lydia 2 mumbled, her head down and her body curled up in her seat.

"Don't think I won't slap you when we get to our room," Mama hissed at Lydia 2. Corporal punishment was illegal everywhere for everyone, but hitting clones in private was an everyday, unspoken practice.

Lydia 3 looked out the windows of the vehicle and marveled at the ancient buildings meticulously maintained by the caretakers, who lived in the town as people did in ages past—no power, primitive technology such as fire ovens in which they cooked food, harvested from small fields and herds of sheep and goats. Outside the city center and the fields, the rest of the area was given over to the lush, tropical-like Mediterranean wildness of palm trees and fragrant flowers.

The Lydias and their mother all stayed in a single room in a brick building with glassless windows, a wooden door and a dirt floor. The caretakers of the building treated the group well, serving them handmade flatbread, vegetables and goat meat with dates on the side for dinner that evening.

With no electronic entertainment to access, and with no electric lighting in the town, Mama ordered the girls to go to bed: A full day of activities would begin with sunrise the next day. They all slept in small, wooden beds, each draped with a net connected to the ceiling to protect the sleepers from biting insects. The two clones lay in beds next to each other; their mother and their original were in beds on the other side of the room. Unaccustomed to going to sleep so early, the clones held a conversation in whispers.

"I learned about cave people at school," Lydia 2 grumbled. "Now Mama has us living like them."

"Yeah, it's so dirty here, just dirty!" Lydia 3 responded. "And dark! Whoo! You can't see anything, not even your hand in front of your face! I didn't know it could get that dark."

"Well, I guess that's what it's like without any lights," Lydia 2 said. She paused for a moment, and then said, "At least in the Outlands, they treat everybody the same."

"Yeah, we all got to squat over a hole in the ground when we have to go to the lavatory!" Lydia 3 said with a snicker.

"I'm serious," Lydia 2 said. "I mean, there's no separate anything here—no separate rooms, no separate travel, the caretakers treat us all nice—we're all the same here, all living like cave people together." She paused again and then added, "I almost wish I could live here."

"What?" Lydia 3 said. "I thought you hated it here."

"I don't like all of us in one room and not having a toilet," Lydia 2 said. "But I might could give that up to live somewhere where everybody is treated the same."

Lydia 2 took a longer pause, and then she said, "Though in a way, it's still the same. They may treat everybody the same in the Outlands, but only originals are allowed to live here."

Lydia 3's seat vibrated suddenly and strongly, jolting her out of her sleep. As the vibration was an alert so sleepers and 'net visor wearers would know that the plane had landed, she quickly pulled off her visor, rubbed the sleep out of her eyes and rose up to join the passengers who were disembarking for Australia.

A day later, the Lydias and two indigenous caretakers were traveling from the temperate south of the continent, through its desert heart, to its tropical northern edge. The vehicle they rode in was large, block-shaped and ruggedly built on the outside, equipped with gigantic, deep-tread tires. Inside the cabin of the vehicle, the travelers sat in cushioned seats that could swivel for a complete turn and recline almost horizontally for sleeping. The vehicle provided drinking water and a lavatory, and it was well stocked with food and other provisions for the weeklong journey.

Lydia 3 was glad for the comfort of the land vehicle, even though living in close quarters with three other people was a bit of a strain. She was not looking forward to the rough lodging at Kakadu, sacred land of the indigenous Australians, where they would be sleeping outdoors and carrying a small portable lavatory to ensure that non-resident waste was not left on the land.

As on the shuttle flight, Lydia 2 barely spoke to Lydia 3 on this part of the journey. Lydia 2 sat in one of the front two seats behind the driver. Across from her sat the other caretaker, a woman with deep brown skin and shockingly white hair. The woman had just the barest hint of lines around her eyes, Lydia 3 thought, but there were plenty of procedures available to eliminate the signs of aging. However, people who chose not to let their faces age didn't let their hair age, so for Lydia 3 the woman was strange and intriguing to behold.

The woman kept up a steady patter of narrative on indigenous history and culture, as well as the more interesting sights on their journey to Kakadu. Lydia 2 was silent though most of the woman's talk, but she looked attentive, turning her seat to face the woman, looking out the windows and nodding when the woman pointed at animals and notable natural landmarks such as rock formations.

Like the caretakers at Tanjah, the woman and the male driver seemed folksy and friendly, treating both outsider guests equally warmly, even though neither of the Lydias said much to the caretakers or each other. Lydia 3 figured that Lydia 2 decided it was unsafe to talk with her clone sister around anyone, even the simple-living caretakers of the Outlands.

For 10 to 12 hours a day, the driver took the vehicle across a long northbound ancient road that was often overgrown with vegetation and strewn with rocks. The vehicle's large tires and sophisticated drive system could handle most obstacles, though once or twice he had to stop driving to get out of the vehicle and use some old-looking power tools Lydia 3 couldn't identify to cut through branches or break up and move larger stones.

In the evenings, while the summer sun was still in the sky, the driver would simply stop on the road—there were no other vehicles that they had to worry about blocking—so he could have dinner with his companion and the passengers and then recline in his seat to sleep once the sun set.

Lydia 3 had a hard time sleeping when the vehicle was still; during the day, the hum of the vehicle in motion and even the rocking movements as it rolled over rough terrain had the effect of lulling her to sleep. This was an effect she didn't want—her eyes couldn't get their fill of the wild and varied Australian land and its wildlife that often literally crossed the vehicle's path: dingoes, wallabies, snakes, so many of the animals Lydia 3 had seen only in holo-videos.

There was so much to see during the day, but blinding night enveloped the vehicle after the sun set. The caretakers automatically took sundown as their signal to wind down and sleep. There were no 'net viewers on board the vehicle, just an old audio communicator device that the caretakers used to check in with some others about their trip progress and other news. When the caretakers dimmed the lights at the front of the cabin, Lydia 2 would pull the 'net visor from her bag and put it on, pushing her seat back and dimming the light above her seat. Lydia 3 was left to sit or lie awake, listening to the night sounds of the wilderness, her mind shifting from fitful drowsiness to startled wakefulness until the caretakers woke with the sunrise, ate their first meal and then started up the vehicle. Lydia 2, still reclined with the 'net visor on her face, wouldn't stir until near the midmorning.

Halfway through the trip to the north, riding through desert lands scattered with low, dry brush during the late afternoon, the woman caretaker noted, "We're gonna be bypassing the road to Ularu soon."

"We're passing by Ularu?" Lydia 3 asked, perking up from another unwanted nap.

"We're not passing right by it," the woman replied with the twangy speech she and the driver shared. "About another 30 kilometers, we'll be at the turning point where if you go west there it is."

The thought of seeing the great red rock at the center of the continent excited Lydia 3. "Why don't we go there?" she proposed.

Lydia 2 asked the woman, "How far is Ularu from the main road?"

"Oh, about 250 kilometers," she said.

Lydia 2 sighed. "That's about three hours, isn't it?"

"Oh yeah," the driver chimed in. "And we'd have a bit of a walk to Ularu after that. No motorized vehicles allowed within the sacred land all around it."

"Well, we're not going," Lydia 2 said. "This trip is long enough as it is without a detour."

But it's Ularu! Lydia 3 screamed in her head. Taking a breath, she said, "We could go there on the way back from Kakadu, after we do what we need to do for Lydia."

Lydia 2's eyes narrowed and her mouth shrunk into a tight frown. "Lydia, I said no."

Lydia 3 huffed and sat back in her seat.

In a clearing ringed by eucalypts with perching red-tailed black cockatoos, the Lydias stood in the late afternoon sun. The caretakers had guided them to this place in Kakadu and then left them to wait about 500 meters away, close enough to reach the women quickly if needed but far away enough to give them privacy.

The cockatoo chatter and the rustling of the tree leaves were the only sounds as the Lydias faced each other, standing about two paces apart. Lydia 2 held the bio-box—the original's remains—in her hands. Lydia 3 took a deep breath, taking in this moment of solitude to reveal her emotions. Her tears followed, flowing freely without Lydia 2 trying to wipe them away.

Lydia 2 started to crumple the bio-box, squeezing it with her spread fingers.

"Stop!" Lydia 3 cried out. "Hold on!"

"What?" Lydia 2 said, her head snapping up.

"I want to say goodbye…I want to say—something!" Lydia 3 gasped.

A quick sigh left Lydia 2's lips. "Then say something," she answered.

Lydia 3 blinked her wet eyes and sniffed. "Don't you want to say something?" she asked. "Something for Lydia? Something for our sister!" The last words came out in chokes, and then the tears flowed fast, joined by sobs.

"You say something, Lydia," Lydia 2 said quietly. "You say something."

Lydia 3 wiped her face with her hands and forearm and snorted hard. With a big swallow, she said, "Lydia, I, I—you were the best big sister…I, love you, forever…I, can't believe I'm never, ever going to see you or talk to you or hear you talk or laugh or anything ever…" She ran out of breath and had to pause. "I miss you so much.

I miss you. I love you." Lydia 3 dropped her head and took rough breaths, exhausted in body and mind.

Lydia 2 resumed crushing the bio-box. Lydia 3 looked up. "You're not going to say anything?" Lydia 3 pled.

"No," Lydia 2 said, continuing to compress the bio-box, creating a powdery white cloud that emanated from her hands and dissipated in the air. Shaking the talc-light remains off her hands, she added, "It's not like Lydia can hear us. She's dead. She's gone."

Lydia 3 felt slapped in the face with her clone sister's bluntness. "How could you be so cold?" she shouted. "It's like you don't care!" Lydia 3 looked at Lydia 2—her clone sister was calm, composed and dry-eyed. "You're not even crying—you haven't cried at all!" Lydia 3's face got hot with the realization. "You haven't cried one tear since—since Lydia—I don't even think you cried for her the day she got hurt!"

"I don't have to cry to be sad," Lydia 2 replied. "Or to prove to you that I'm grieving."

"But she's...she was our big sister!" Lydia 3 insisted. "Our original! Without her, there's no us. You, you..."

"I don't have to be like you!" Lydia 2 growled through her teeth. "I've never wanted to be like you or Lydia—you know that. And now I don't have to. I don't have to be a clone sister—I don't have to be a clone. I can be an individual—an original. And I can do, be and feel whatever the hell I want!"

"You sound like you're glad she's dead!" Lydia 3 spat out. Her rage made her body shake as she glared at Lydia 2.

Lydia 2 raised her chin and pursed her lips. Slowly, deliberately, she said "What I sound like, what I feel, what I think, what I do is not your business. I'm an original. You're a clone."

"You are not an original!" Lydia 3 shouted. "What you are is insane! You're not Lydia! You're her clone!" She moved closer to Lydia 2, feeling an urge to hit her clone sister.

"You want to tell people that?" Lydia 2 said, staring Lydia 3 in the eyes. "Go ahead. Go tell the caretakers, but then they might not care. Then go tell when we leave the Outlands. Tell people what we both have done—so they can destroy us both."

With that, Lydia 3's emotions went from hot to frozen. Her heart beat fast and hard, but her skin felt numb. Time slowed to a standstill in her head.

"Please talk to Lydia. She thinks you don't care about her."

"Did she say that?"

"Yeah. She said you don't care about us."

"I love her! And she says I don't care about her? She doesn't know how good she has it, how good her life is because she's my clone! I was going to just let her have her little pouting spell and just leave her alone, like I always do, but you know what? You're right—I am going to talk to her. We're going to have this out right now. This is between her and me. I don't need you trying to mediate or hold us back. It's all coming out, and let the chips fall where they may!"

Lydia 2 slowly stepped toward Lydia 3, who couldn't move.

"I'm ready to die," Lydia 2 said softly. "Are you?"

Lydia 3, her mind shut down by the cold shock, could not answer.

Lydia 2 grabbed Lydia 3 and pulled her into her arms. "You don't want to die," Lydia 2 whispered. "You don't want me to die. So let's live."

Lydia 2 tapped her left wrist while holding Lydia 3, and then said, "The caretakers are on their way now."

This excerpt was published (in slightly different form) in *The Future of Us: An Anthology* (Charlotte Bailey & Florence Okoye, editors), Afrofutures_UK (July 4, 2016).

https://issuu.com/afrofutures_uk/docs/afrofutures_uk_anthology_issue

Notes

Secret Insurrection, from which these published excerpts are derived, is a novel draft that I am currently revising.

For more information about my work, connect with me online:
• Twitter: @blackathenapm
• LinkedIn: www.linkedin.com/in/stephani-m-booker
• Goodreads: www.goodreads.com/athenapm

Thank you for your support!

Stephani Maari Booker
Writer, editor, publisher